J

3/2007

The
FOOT
BOOK

By
Dr. Seuss

A Bright & Early Book

RANDOM HOUSE / NEW YORK

This title was originally cataloged by the Library of Congress as follows:
Seuss, Dr. The foot book. Random House [© 1968]
unp. illus. (Bright and early books for beginning beginners)
Text and pictures tell about many kinds of feet—front feet, back feet, red feet,
black feet, slow feet, quick feet, trick feet, sick feet, etc.
Author's full name: Theodor Seuss Geisel
1 Foot I Title ISBN 0-394-80937-8 (trade) ISBN 0-394-90937-2 (lib. bdg.)

Printed in the United States of America   **74**

Left foot
Left foot

Right foot
Right

Feet in the morning

Feet at night

Left foot

Left foot

Left foot

Right

Wet foot

Dry foot

High foot

Low foot

Front feet

Back feet

Red feet

Black feet

Left foot   Right foot

Feet   Feet   Feet

How many, many
feet you meet.

Slow feet

Quick feet

Trick feet

Sick feet

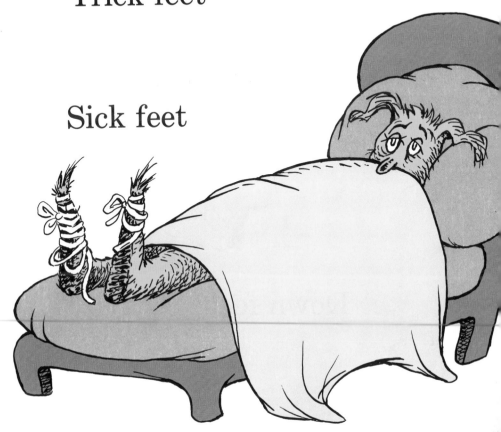

Up feet

Down feet

Here come clown feet.

Small feet

Big feet

Here come pig feet.

His feet

Her feet

Fuzzy fur feet

In the house,
and on the street,

how many, many
feet you meet.

Up in the air feet

Over a chair feet

More and more feet

Twenty-four feet

Here come
more and more . . . .

. . . . and more feet!

Left foot.   Right foot.

Feet. Feet. Feet.

Oh, how many
feet you meet!